Mutton Soup

More Adventures of Johnny Mutton

Stories and pictures by James Proimos

Harcourt, Inc.
Orlando Austin New York San Diego Toronto London

www.HarcourtBooks.com

Library of Congress Cataloging-in-Publication Data
Proimos, James.
Mutton soup: more adventures of Johnny Mutton/stories and pictures by James Proimos.
p. cm.
Summary: Presents more humorous stories about Johnny Mutton,
the young sheep raised as a regular boy.
[1. Sheep—Fiction. 2. Humorous stories.] I. Title.
PZ7.P9432Mu 2004
[E]—dc21 2003000038
ISBN 0-15-216772-2

First edition

A C E G H F D B

Manufactured in China

The illustrations in this book were first drawn with a pen,
then colorized in Adobe Photoshop.
The display type was set in Textile.
The text type was set in Lemonade.
Color separations by Colourscan Co. Pte. Ltd., Singapore
Manufactured by South China Printing Company, Ltd., China
This book was printed on totally chlorine-free Stora Enso Matte paper.
Production supervision by Sandra Grebenar and Ginger Boyer
Designed by Barry Age

For Karen Grove

The Stories

MUTTON SOUP IS 100% MELTED VANILLA ICE CREAM WITH A CHERRY ON TOP.

In the Dark

Johnny was playing a neighborhood game of hide-and-seek.
READY OR NOT, HERE I COME!
YIPES!

Johnny ducked into a nearby closet.

It was dark.

He wasn't all that fond of the dark.

LA, LA, LA, LA.

He sings when he's nervous.

Then he starts talking to himself.

I'M NOT AFRAID!
I'M NOT AFRAID!
I'M NOT AFRAID!

HEY, SOMEONE ELSE IS HIDING IN HERE, TOO!

YEP.

AND YOU'RE AFRAID OF THE DARK, TOO!

YOU GOT THAT RIGHT.

I'M NOT AFRAID OF ANYTHING ELSE.
OH, I AM.

I'M AFRAID OF BEES!

AND DENTURES!

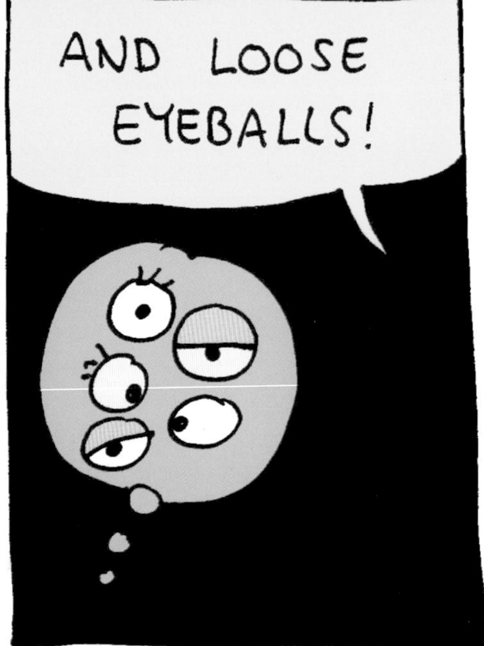
AND LOOSE EYEBALLS!

I'M AFRAID OF THOSE THINGS, TOO!

HOLD MY HAND!
HOLD MINE!

I'M GLAD WE'RE IN HERE TOGETHER.

FOUND YOU!

JOHNNY MUTTON!

MANDY DINKUS!

AUUGGHH!

MUTTON PUDDING HAS NO LUMPY BITS, BUT IT DOES HAVE A CHERRY ON TOP.

Bottoms Up

One day Momma said . . .
I LOVE YOU, JOHNNY, BUT YOU DON'T HAVE VERY GOOD DINNER MANNERS.

She was right.

Johnny always put his napkin on his head instead of in his lap.

He said "pronto" when he was supposed to say "please."

He hid Momma's plate whenever she left the table.

THIS JUST WON'T DO. I'M SENDING YOU FOR A LESSON WITH MS. BOTTOMS.
HER NAME IS MS. BOTTOMS? HA!

THERE IS NOTHING FUNNY ABOUT MS. BOTTOMS. SHE'S A MANNERS EXPERT.
DOESN'T THAT MAKE HER NAME EVEN FUNNIER?
KIND OF.

The next day Johnny went for his lesson with Ms. Bottoms.

DON'T TALK WITH YOUR MOUTH FULL.
WHAT?

NOW, WHY IS YOUR NAPKIN ON YOUR HEAD?
IT LOOKED SILLY STUFFED UNDER MY ARM.

That was the last straw.

Ms. Bottoms took Johnny home.

That night at dinner,
Johnny was the perfect gentleman.
I AM SO IMPRESSED!
IF HE HAD A PINKY IT WOULD BE EXTENDED
CAN'T TALK. MOUTH FULL.
NAPKIN IN LAP
And it was fun.

And that very same night, Ms. Bottoms
and her poodle, Mr. Tooshy,
had an equally fun dinner.
WHAT?
WOOF!

MUTTON GRAVY
IS THE HOT
MAPLE SYRUP
THAT GOES OVER
THE PANCAKES
THAT HAVE A
CHERRY ON
TOP.

For the Record

Most people weren't sophisticated enough to appreciate a great sitter.

So Johnny decided to set a world record while sitting.

Gloria Crust liked the idea so much, she asked to join him.

For days all they talked about was setting the record.

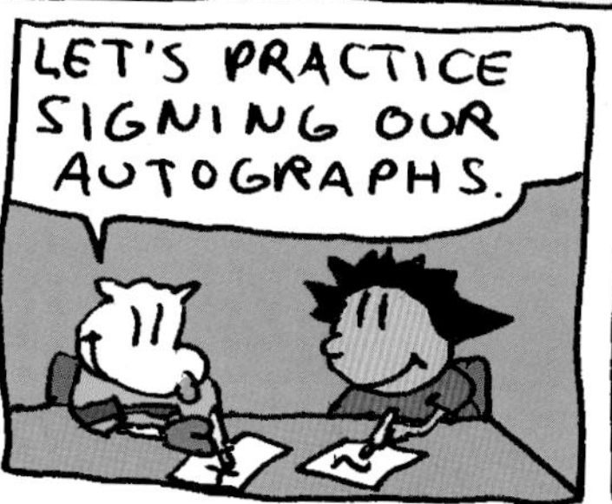

Finally the big day came.
The start
Going up
And up
And up
And up
And up
And down
Down
Down

Their first ride was wild.
First turn
The loop
Second turn
Up again
Down again
Another loop
The last turn
Comin' in
All done!

Gloria couldn't wait to ride again . . .
until she saw Johnny's face.

THANKS FOR MAKING ME FEEL GOOD ABOUT FEELING BAD.
NO PROBLEM.
GOO. GOO.
NICE SITTING.
LIKEWISE, SISTA!
BAA BAA.
SOMETIMES JUST HAVING FUN IS MORE IMPORTANT THAN A SILLY RECORD.
GET ME OFF THIS THING. I'M SICK.

MUTTON PIE
IS NOTHING BUT
A WHOLE LOT
OF CHERRIES
IN A BOWL
WITH A
CHERRY ON TOP.

My Dinner with Dinkus

There was only one word to describe the way Johnny felt about Mandy Dinkus . . . and that word was . . .

GRRRR.

Johnny and Mandy had the terrible habit of challenging each other to contests at the drop of a hat.

One day Johnny came home and said . . .

I WOULD NEVER HURT A BUG.
DING DONG
YOU KNOW ME.

GO AWAY!
I'M PLAYING MY FLUTE!
YOU HEARD THE MAN!

IT'S JOHNNY MUTTON AND HIS MOMMA.
NOW HE'LL NEVER LET US IN.

But Mutton was wrong. The door burst open.
COME ON IN! COME ON IN!
I'VE HEARD SO MUCH ABOUT YOU!
It was Mr. Dinkus.

Mr. Dinkus invited Momma and Johnny to have dinner with Mandy and him.

Johnny needed to come up with a good idea fast.

He did.

DID YOU ALL KNOW THAT MOMMA THINKS THE TUBA IS THE GREATEST INSTRUMENT IN THE WORLD?

Mandy jumped right in.

MY DADDY SAYS THE FLUTE IS THE GREATEST!

HA! YOU'VE GOT TO BE KIDDING!

TUBA!
FLUTE!
TUBA!
FLUTE!
TUBA!
FLUTE!
TUBA!
FLUTE!

THAT'S IT! I CHALLENGE YOU TO A MUSIC-OFF!
YOU'RE ON, MISSY!

Momma and Johnny left without even eating their dessert.
HA! HA!
HA! SEE HOW HARD IT IS NOT TO CHALLENGE SOMEONE?
I NOTICED YOU AND MANDY WORKED WELL TOGETHER, THOUGH.
HA!
TRUE!
HA!
But they laughed the whole way home.

A MUTTON SANDWICH IS TWO CUPCAKES WITH A CUPCAKE IN BETWEEN AND A CHERRY ON TOP.

Old Man Stagglemyer

One day Johnny was walking and listening and walking and listening to the Winslow triplets tell one of their famous long stories.

OH MY!
WHERE ARE WE?
LOST, PERHAPS?
ACTUALLY, WE'VE ONLY BEEN WALKING AROUND THE BLOCK.
147 TIMES.
148.

OH, REALLY! WELL, I'VE NEVER SEEN THAT HOUSE BEFORE!
YIPES!

AT SOME POINT WE CROSSED THE STREET, BECAUSE THAT'S OLD MAN STAGGLEMYER'S HOUSE.
OLD MAN WHO-ELMYER?

HE'S SO OLD HE HAS GREEN TEETH!

HE'S SO OLD HE HAS YELLOW EYES!

HE'S SO OLD HE SMELLS LIKE CHEESE!

The next day Johnny got Momma and they went to see Old Man Stagglemyer.

Old Man Stagglemyer answered the door.
GET OUT!
WHAT IS THIS GUY, PERMANENTLY GRUMPY?
GREEN TEETH.
YELLOW EYES.
DOES ANYONE SMELL CHEESE?

Johnny took off!
OLD PEOPLE ARE SCARY! OLD PEOPLE ARE SCARY!

Johnny ran right into Old Woman Stagglemyer, who was planting tulips.
AUUGH!
HAVE A TULIP.
SORRY TO RUN INTO YOU.
WHAT BEAUTIFUL EYES.
I GET A WONDERFUL FEELING FROM HER.
SHE SMELLS LIKE FRESH BREAD.
WARM SMILE.

Old Woman Stagglemyer and Johnny became great friends. In fact, they skateboard together every Friday!

And every so often,
Old Man Stagglemyer joins them.

Where Are They Now?

The soup is gone.

The pie has disappeared.

Who knows where the pudding went.

The gravy isn't here.

The sandwich has vanished.

Where's Johnny?

He's in bed with a tummy ache.
You gotta love him.